THE GIRL AND THE ELEPHANT

The Girl and the Elephant

Nicole de Cock

TRICYCLE PRESS

Berkeley/Toronto

For Bibi, faithful feline friend.
You will always be with me.

This is the girl. She often goes to the zoo.

She goes to see the animals, wishing there were no bars between them.
She visits the birds…

and the apes...

but most of all, she loves the elephant.

Sometimes she brings along a carrot.

At first the elephant is afraid to take it.

He really loves carrots though. So he comes just within reach.

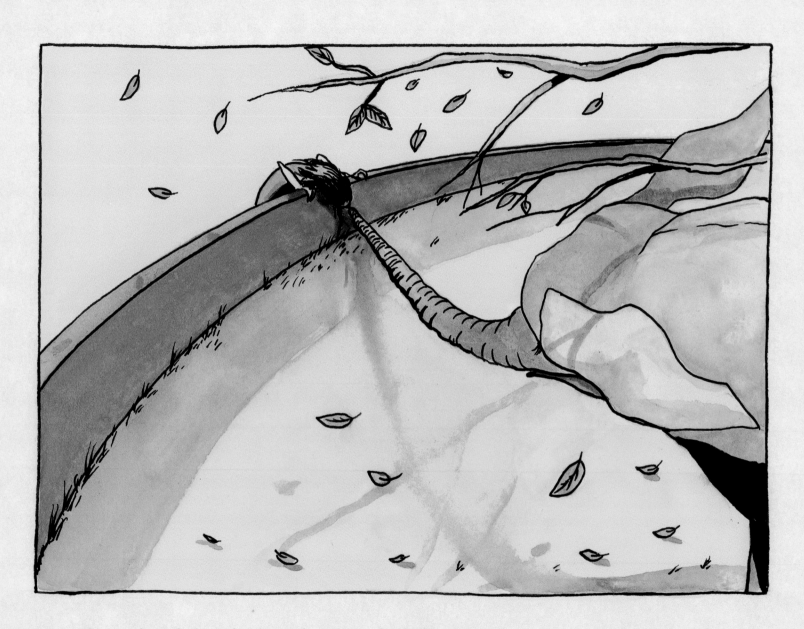

The girl and the elephant become friends.

They love being together.

Sometimes they play an elephant game.

And sometimes they play a girl game.

And then one day, the elephant is gone.

Back to Africa, says the caretaker.

Why are you so sad? asks the swift.

The elephant has gone off to Africa.

Can you help me?

Good-bye! Have a safe flight! the girl calls.

The swift sets out on a long journey.

He's off to Africa, to find the elephant.

Big bird, have you seen an elephant?

I'm looking for an elephant—big, gray, with a long trunk.

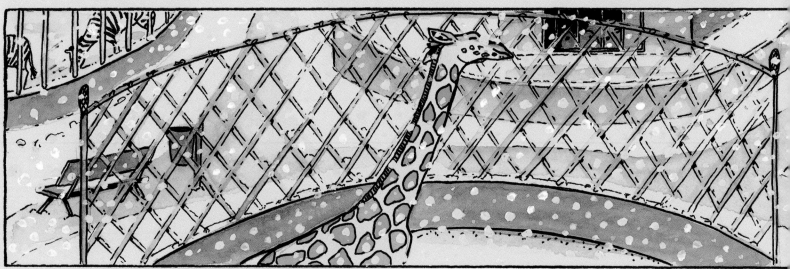

And while the swift continues searching warm Africa,

back home, at the zoo, it is very cold.

The girl still visits anyway because she loves the animals so.

But she really misses the elephant.

Does he miss her too?

And how is he doing there?

As the first rays of sunshine chase the winter away,

the swift returns with good news.

All summer long, the girl thinks about the elephant.

And then she decides.

Autumn is coming, and the girl and the swift are going on a trip.

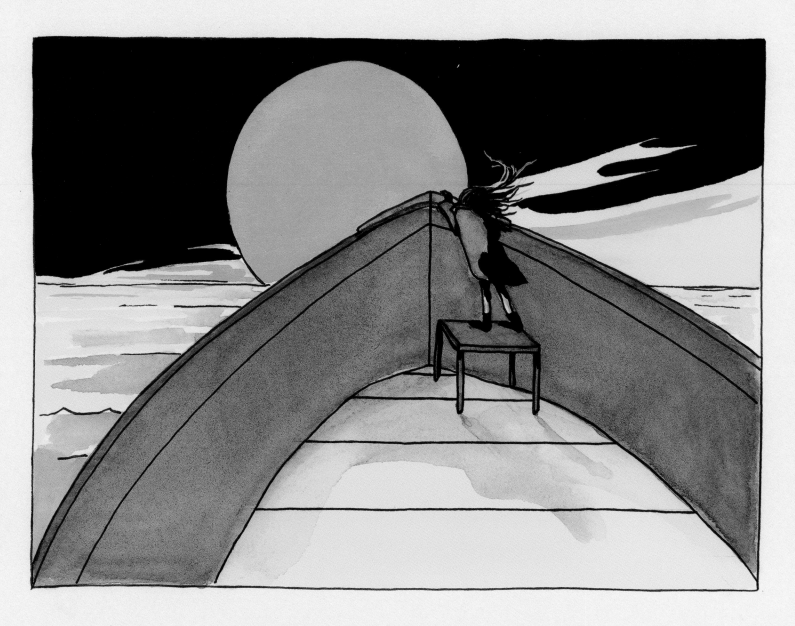

To Africa!

First a huge distance by boat.

And then by airplane.

They arrive after a long journey.

But Africa is so big!

Have you seen my elephant?

The girl searches day and night.

And then…

finally, together again!

And the whole winter long, they play girl games.

And they play elephant games.

© 2003 by Nicole de Cock
© 2003 by Uitgeverij J.H. Gottmer/H.J.W. Becht BV, Haarlem,
the Netherlands
Translation by Lorraine T. Miller/Epicycles, Amsterdam
Originally published under the title: *Het meisje en de olifant*.

Tricycle Press
a little division of Ten Speed Press
P.O. Box 7123
Berkeley, California 94707
www.tenspeed.com

Design by Betsy Stromberg
Typeset in Bembo
The illustrations in this book were rendered in watercolor and
black ink.

Library of Congress Cataloging-in-Publication Data

Cock, Nicole de.
  [Het meisje en de olifant English]
  The girl and the elephant / Nicole de Cock ; [translation by
Lorraine T. Miller].
     p. cm.
  Summary: A girl becomes good friends with the elephant she
visits at the zoo, and when he returns to Africa, she wonders if
she will ever see him again.
  ISBN 1-58246-133-3
  [1. Elephants—Fiction. 2. Animals—Fiction. 3. Zoos—Fiction.]
I. Miller, Lorraine T. II. Title.
  PZ7.C639779Gi 2004
  [E]—dc22
                                        2003028257

First Tricycle Press printing, 2004
Printed in Singapore

1 2 3 4 5 6 — 08 07 06 05 04